Tourniquet

Tourniquet

Visions from 'Tarin Row'

Larry B. Bachman

Printed in the United States of America
ISBN 978-1-64133-933-9 (sc)
ISBN 978-1-64133-934-6 (e)
ISBN 978-1-64133-935-3 (hc)

2024.09.24

This book is printed on acid-free paper.

Blue Ink Media Solutions
1111B S Governors Ave
STE 7582 Dover,
DE 19904

www.blueinkmediasolutions.com

Before Alpha, beyond Omega, the Creator walked among the stars. He spoke into existence the earth, felt the warmth of the sun and was pleased with the vast beauty of His creations. He bore witness to the frailty of flesh, felt physical pain and emptied Himself to quench the anguish of the fallen souls.

There were messengers sent to lighten the burdens of the people of earth, but most did not hear or take up their call. The messengers were called fools or worse; tortured and murdered. The King witnessed his Father's messages distorted, twisted and spun to fill the needs of those most powerful.

The King again looked down upon the creation of Earth. With crown on high He gazed at the Father and raised His voice to plead the case. It was time again to return, and time once more to send messengers.

Now who are you this, but mere dust of a troubled soul? By-product of tortured dreams, broken hearts and broken backs from your endless toil, now are grist for the grinding wheel. Sanctuary is waiting as the wafting prayers of despair are heard, "I am come to answer", is His reply.

Table of Contents

G. T. O. and 'The Break'

This is me and here I sit or what's left of me. I was born thirty-five years ago into a lower-middle class family in Breaker's Mills. From coal mines, trucks brought ore to the breakers and then it was loaded on the coal train; that is how the town got its name. Back then it was a one store, one garage and one church country town at the end of a lazy, dusty Appalachian road. Much of the small town's dirt is buried now including many of its older resident's selective memories. One has to dig down deep past black dust, gravel and clay to find truth these days.

It is said that everyone gets what they want in the end whether they know it or not. Admittedly that understanding is most times beyond an individual's immediate understanding. Aware or not, wishes do come true and the soul knows its way to travel. So perhaps this story is an affirmation of outcome to someone's secret wish. There's no way to tell the stories of all those who have come prior without them sounding like admissions of guilt. By telling their stories I include my own. Maybe they are simply just that; confessions.

We all look to a higher being in order to triumph over whatever trial lay before us. Good does not always overcome evil. Sometimes the dark side slips through the better venues of our nature.

Where does the story begin you ask? At '*The Break*' of course, as the locals call it. It lies over there past the bars I'm sittin behind; over there beyond that second hill you'll find it. Make a right at the sharp left bend off the main highway, take the first left off the secondary, go about a mile and a quarter on the dirt road and if you come to a stop sign… you probably missed it.

Couldn't miss '*The Break*' if I tried… been down that road. Walked it before I could ride, biked it before I could drive, and hopefully won't die on it before my time. Memories…

they're here in my brain, locked inside like the familiar smells and sounds of the old country church. Week after week we walked less than a quarter mile to that sanctuary. At the age of twelve I committed my life to the Lord. That night I flew home, riding on the wings of a dove. It was the curtain call for my age of innocence where everything within my small world seemed possible. I was the boy in a bubble. But how long could I last within the insulation of naivety?

Strangely and oddly for me back then, and being the African American that I am, I believed normalcy was based upon the lives of Ozzie and Harriet. We set our clocks to the Little Beaver Cleaver family, Dennis the Menace and the neighborly Mr. Wilson. The only evil that tapped on the gate of the white picket fence back then was when "Outer Limits" and "The Twilight Zone" would take control of the small Zenith that sat on the stand in the living room. And that only happened once a week on Thursday night.

It took two paychecks and a lot of hard work to keep our family goin. My brother and I were raised mostly by our maternal grandmother. Grandma would try to keep us in tow but every now and again I would slipstream into the "*Outer Limits*" side of my nature. "The devil is in you today", she would warn.

Grandma was a good, God fearing woman who raised a family of seven through the Great Depression. She entrusted all to; "Therefore here by the grace of God go I", she would say. She was gifted as I later found out from my momma. It was inferred that grandma had some sort of intuitive precognition. "She could see things"… That's all momma would say, "And things were drawn to her".

My thought at the time was… "Things?… What sort of things?" An answer to that question was never given me.

Oh wow! Where are my manners? Momma would smack me if she knew I hadn't properly introduced myself. I'm G. T. O. and I need to tell you why I am sittin here in this jailhouse. Oh man… you need to know that! And you can't figure out where you're going unless you know where you been, right? And where we are headed, now that's the thing. You're probably thinkin my name is as kewl black as you can get right… G. T. O. yeah man, like the car? Got it?

That's kinda the way I got my name and what this dealeeo is all about. My poppa liked those old classic cars and when I was born he thought since his last name is Owens, yeah… you get the picture… George Taylor fit like a glove. So here I sit yours truly, G. T. O., George Taylor Owens. And I'm glad to meet ya!

Oh… how I got here? Let's start at the best part. My poppa had been in the 82nd out of Fort Bragg and was a radio man who liked fixin things. When he ended his tour of military service pop opened a radio and TV repair shop in the bigger town close by. That's where I went to school and started playing football. Throwing and running the ball came easy to me. Girls said I naturally had good hands, but hey, let's not get ahead of ourselves, that being a whole 'nother story.

Let me tell you man, out there under the lights there's nothing like havin your name called out by the fans. Yeah, I can still hear em yellin, "Go! Go! G-T-O!… Go! Go! G-T-O!" and that being a long time ago… still right here in my head though, but might as well be never-ever-land now.

Quarterback was my position in high school and everyone told me it would take me to the top. But man, I cannot forget that constantly I was beat over the head by my parents tellin me that learnin was above everything else.

"George T", momma would say, "First; don't let color stand in your way son, you can do anything you want to, all you have to do is study hard and stay outta trouble. Second; play football, but sports ain't gonna carry you son if you get hurt or help you when the world starts forgettin about who you was."

My parents pushed me and I listened. I did everything they told me to do. Always I was on the honor roll, and athletically I was better than most, and I didn't hang out. This nose was always in the books. When I wasn't studyin I was sweepin floors at dads shop. He worked hard too; sometimes sixteen hours a day. It was for the family he said; "I do it so we can all have a better life."

But I knew he was watchin me. I knew how proud he was of me even though he never came right out and said it. How'd he show it? He was at every game… maybe not for every kick-off, but he managed to make time to be there. Whenever he could he'd bring my little brother and momma along too. Believe me when I say I could hear momma callin out from the stands. Whew!… Right or wrong she'd try to keep'em honest!

I asked momma one time why poppa never said much and you know what she told me, "You know George T. your daddy loves you and your brother more than anything else in the whole world. He just can't show it like other folks do. His daddy was a real hard drinkin man and never gave up love for anybody or any-thing. It was like his daddy cursed the world for his being born and beat on his wife somethin terrible too. That's why your poppa left and joined the army before he was legal. He said he had to get out before he did something real bad to his daddy for hurtin his momma."

After hearing what my momma told me I came to the conclusion that poppa truly did love us, but he was afraid. He lived in fear that our love, and our lives were so fragile that if he hugged us too much, or loved us too much, we might break apart and disappear.

During my senior year in high school I was offered a football scholarship from one of the big colleges. Hold on, I know what you are thinkin… nahh, it wasn't to play quarterback. They said I had good hands and was so quick they pegged me for a wide-receiver. You know it worked. I was only halfway through my junior year when I had the pro's knocking on my door. Let me tell you somethin, get me the ball and this boy could move. I had some wheels.

It was in my third year of college when suddenly from out of nowhere the wheels came off and the gravy train I was on derailed. Knowing where you're headed… now that's as I said, the thing.

Genesis 4:9-13 (KJV) *And the Lord said unto Cain; "Where is Abel thy brother?" And he said, "I know not: Am I my brother's keeper?"*

And the Lord said, "What hast thou done? The voice of thy brother's blood crieth out to me from the ground.

And now art thou cursed from the earth, which hath opened her mouth to receive thy brother's blood from thy hand;

When thou tillest the ground, it shall not henceforth yield unto thee its strength; a fugitive and a vagabond shalt thou be in the earth.

And Cain said unto the Lord; "My punishment is greater than I can bear."

Blind Sided

Finding me shrouded in disbelief, standing one last time before the man who had been my biggest fan and my silent hero was numbing. But as I touched his cold hand, I leaned over and told him that I loved him one last time, stark reality washed over me like Noah's flood. In trepidation I walked back to my momma and brother sitting in the front of the funeral parlor. Placing my arms around them, we cried and I held on for dear life to the only real love and truth I had ever known.

After the burial ceremony we went back to our house. Many people showed up who knew my father offering their condolences. All sat around saying nice things, giving out pleasantries, eating from platters and desserts brought by aunts, uncles and people I had never met before.

Then it was all over. There we were, left alone in silence, oddly numb and dumb, not finding the words, not having any more to say; momma, my not so little brother and me.

"It was nice, don't ya think… the ceremony I mean, and the Preacher did say some nice things about your poppa", momma said trying to start conversation in order to break the roaring silence.

"He's dead momma, what can anybody say but nice things", I said in a not so nice smug tone. "G. T." exclaimed my brother Sammy, "That's no way to be talkin to momma."

"He's grievin'sall Sammy", said momma being the consummate peace keeper, "Let it out boys. Believe me I know how much it hurts."

Paying little attention to momma's last comment I asked, "I didn't ask you before momma and maybe now is not the time either but, didn't anybody see anything? What kind of a car hit poppa? Where are the cops? But most of all, what the hell was he doing walkin on the side of that damn highway late at night?"

My brother spoke up, "The gas gauge doesn't work… the one in that old van of his is bust. He ran out of gas. So, he grabbed his gas can and went walkin to fetch some and BANG… hit and run. Seems he could fix anything for anybody, but the things he owns, he lets go to hell."

Our momma now spoke out, "Your FATHER put all he had into making a better life for you boys… he invested in you—not in THINGS, innate objects that didn't mean anything to him. You boys were his investment in life… his flesh… his blood."

Asking with a too edgy tone, I threw it out there anyway, "And what about you? Momma are you goin back to teachin school now… at your age? Did poppa invest in you? I hope he left you something, because you sure don't know how to fix a TV or a radio?"

Sammy jumped out of his chair and wanted to bust me up as he said, "That's it, darn you G-T-O. …Hell no, this ain't about momma, this is about you ain't it? You are worried about your big time college expenses… and where that money's gonna come from? That's it in a nut ain't it 'Mr. Big Time G. T. O.' most-possible-to-go-pro?"

Honestly and truly, in my head I wasn't even thinkin that. I was really upset at poppa for dyin on us, and thinkin about momma pickin up the pieces. My brother now called me out so what else could a going all pro do… I jumped up and suddenly the two mellow brothers were lookin to get some.

Momma jumped outta her chair and muscled between brother and me. When momma lion got upset she didn't need daddy lion to get the job done… she brought it on.

"Stop this nonsense now! Both of you, stop dissin' your father, Lord rest his soul, and surely stop dissin' me—cause I ain't dead—I'm right here and can hear every word. So sit down and let me do the talkin… and-I-mean-now!"

We obeyed… took our seats eyeballing one another, making little gesture's like you—me outside later. Momma smacked Sammy upside the head and then glared at me asking if I wanted some of the same. I held up my hands and she said, "That's what I thought!"

Rubbing his head my brother glared at me behind momma's back. "Sammy", momma warned, "I can feel you back there." I just sat quietly and could feel the halo shining above my head.

Catching her breath, fanning herself with her hand momma gathered composure and continued, "Oh Lord Jesus be my witness… I am surely gonna speak my mind. Your daddy loved us all, PERIOD. He loved me with all the passion he had and he was a good provider for this family. Can I get an Amen?"

Brother and I concurred, "Amen".

"Thank you both", momma continued, "And without a doubt, as you two can testify, he dearly loved you both. Poppa may have been strict, but he only had your best interests at heart."

"For the record", momma stated. "Now as far as you two are concerned about how I am to make it on my own? The Lord always provides. He provided for Elijah, and he will provide for me, Amen.

Financially for you two there are some things which he set aside. Above and beyond that let me be perectly clear, God gave each of you strong wills, two hands, two feet, two eyes and ears so you can hear and obey your momma. You both got brains, use them! Sammy your poppa left you the shop and store and everything in it. You can work it, sell it—blow all the money—it's yours to do with as you wish."

Momma reached into her purse and threw the keys to Sammy and continued. "I must say that poppa and I had high hopes that one day, surely one of you, would commence to take up the ministry. But that ain't likely now, not without your poppa being here to push the issue."

Looking at me straight from over top of her tortoise shell glasses she paused and then said, "You... George T. seem to be the gifted one, as far as talent goes. Not that I think any less of your brother Sammy, as he has his gifts as well. I believe he has a more stick-to-it business sense and that's why he got the store."

Sammy glared at me, gave a smirk, pointed to his head and nodded up and down. Momma noted that and smacked him again. Sammy recoiled and said, "Come on momma."

"Hmmm—hmmm", momma replied shaking her finger at Sammy.

"Now back to you George T.", Momma firmly stated, "You have a chance at going pro, we know that and boy so do you. I am sure that will take you to the next level IF and I dare say IF you don't get hurt or mess it up in some way, shape or form. So here is what your daddy left you."

Digging into her purse again Momma threw another set of keys to me. She explained and warned us at the same time, "Neither of you boys knew about this… I didn't know either. How could we have seen this all coming? He said when he died it was my decision as to who received what. You know how he liked to tinker with things. I have no idea what the thing is worth George T., same as Sammy and the store. You boys take and do with them as you will."

Slowly turning the keys over in my hand, I looked at the key holder. The metal key ring had a black background but the chrome letters G-T-O called out to me. Throwing around ideas in my head, the only thing I could think of to say, "Momma, you kidding me?"

She said, "WHAT?"

"I mean where did dad hide this thing… and is it what I think it is", I questioned? Momma replied, "Like George Taylor Owens its' got wheels is all your poppa told me." "Where is it", I asked?

Momma said, "He brought it here awhile ago after you went off to college, put it in the back of the garage and it's been sittin there under an old canvas tarp ever since. He'd take it outta the garage, start it up, wash and wax it and put it back, never showed it off or drove it around. You can go look at it if you want. Why… you can do whatever you want, it's yours now."

Sammy looked at his set of keys and then at me. Momma noticed this taking a verbal que, "Oh no we're not boys… we are not goin down envy road because I will slap the sap out of you two and take both those sets of keys and keep it all to myself."

Both of us started laughing and Sammy said, "I was never into cars momma. Besides when Mr. G-T-O goes back to school he'll have the opportunity or need to find someone to keep the passenger seat warm."

"Only with momma's permission", I offered, "Or I could leave it here and allow you to take it out of the garage and rev-up the engine in the driveway. Then you could give it a weekly wash and wax and put it back where it belongs."

"Get out of here both of you", demanded momma, "Take your new toy, go pick up your cousins Teisha and Gregory… take them for some ice cream or something. Get your minds off this old lady for an hour or two—let me relax and breathe."

Its'a Classic

Sammy and I went out the back door and headed for the garage. But first we paused on the back porch and listened. We could hear Momma sobbing mixed with prayers. My brother and I looked at each other as tears welled in our eyes. It tore out our hearts to hear Momma going through this, but we knew that Momma's faith was strong enough to carry her and all of us through this time of mourning.

There sat poppa's old van, faulty gas gauge and all in the yard beside the garage. Felt like I wanted to kick dirt on it or set it on fire. It seemed to hold a foreboding all its own. Like the van itself had something to do with why poppa died in the first place? Sammy and I didn't want to look at it, didn't want to touch it. It could fade away into distant memory and rust-out where it stood for all we cared.

Lifting the roll up garage door, we walked inside. As our eyes adjusted to the light, there it was just as momma said; a tarp with something hidden underneath.

"You first to do the honors", said my brother Sammy. "Thank you and I would be honored", I answered.

Anxiously pulling off the tarp wrap, dust flew everywhere but when it settled there appeared a dark colored, 1967 Pontiac GTO. "Unbelievable", I exclaimed.

"How much do you think it is worth", asked my brother?

"Who cares", was my reply, "Let's get in and ride. Move Momma's car out of the way and I'll start it up."

"Cool", said Sammy, "I don't hope we shock the neighborhood when they see two black dudes in this classic car cruisin around. They'll think we jacked it."

"Who cares", again was my reply, "Let's get in and ride!"

In my mind I could hear a countdown and then, "We have ignition", I spoke out as I turned the key… the engine fired! The start-up was like a series of tiny atomic explosions. It sat there shuddering and uttering its signature throaty purr. Listening closely, I could have sworn the car seemed to cry out to me. Did poppa hear the message as he toiled to put the pieces of this antique together again? Was this the call of a Phoenix ready to burst forth from the shingled roof mausoleum, where it sat idle for the last several years?

Pushing in the clutch I moved the chrome Hurst floor shifter into first and brought the car out into the sunlight. My brother stood in front of the car and shook his head and smiled. He asked dangling his set of keys, "Man, are you sure you don't want the store?"

Answering his question by not saying a word I set the brake, turned off the engine and got out of the car. The midnight blue metal flake came alive in the sunlight. From where you stood the car appeared black but as you moved around the color turned navy blue iridescent. Everything that poppa did to the car was done in perfect detail from the paint and chrome down to the wheels that turned. It was truly a custom classic piece of car art.

"Unlatch the hood man, let's see what poppa put under there", demanded my brother, "not that I know anything about cars but let's take a look anyway."

We opened the hood and stood back and my brother whistled and said, "Four hundred cubic inch ram air, three hundred sixty horses of pure muscle. This ride doesn't just have wheels man you just grew a huge set and sprouted wings too. This is one clean machine. You could eat off the custom chrome air cleaner."

As we leaned underneath the hood of this road rocket our minds could not totally grasp the beauty and significance that rested there. Turning our heads we looked at each other sporting huge grins and I asked, "Shall we ride?"

Visions of watching manned moon rockets taking off from various NASA facilities came to mind. Dreams of going where I or my brother never had gone before danced through my head.

Looking at me, Sammy quickly snapped me out of the daydream, "I think we owe it to poppa not to let another minute pass us by before we take this machine onto the street. Let's ride into our future my brother."

With that being said we closed the hood and jumped into the car, restarted the engine and as I was about to put the car into gear; Momma called out from the back porch to remind us of her intentions for the cars first mission out into daylight, "I called your cousin Teisha and said you would pick her and her little brother Gregory up for some ice cream."

After taking a deep breath I let out some of testosterone filled air which had inflated my head. Through clenched teeth I politely and obediently answered, "Yes momma."

"SShhheeet", commented my brother, "Man if that don't put us on the shelf and damper our day. We might as well put this ride back in the toy box and drive momma's car."

Shrugging my shoulders I put it in gear and slowly pulled out on to the street. As we arrived in front of my aunt's house Teisha and her brother were sitting on the steps waiting for us. "Wow", exclaimed our twelve year old cousin Gregory, "GTO's got himself a GTO!"

Teisha who looked more like twenty-six than sixteen came over and ran her fingers across the side of the car said, "Cool ride GT, you're all hooked up now. How fast does it go?"

Completely put off by her nonsense I said, "Just get in the car girl and stay buckled so you don't get loose. We're supposed to be going for ice cream and back home and that's it."

Teisha gave a pout and said, "Sorry GT, save that hard for the field. I'm not looking for a good licking right now… just some ice cream will do."

Sammy said, "Watch your mouth girl. You're like a cat in heat. You're little brother's sitting right here and you're behavin' like somethin' off the street."

"Chill dude… I'm just goofin on ya…" said Teisha trying to skate around the obvious.

"You absorbing too much of that TV brain wash junk", warned Sammy, "….it's affectin how you thinking things outta be, not how it is. You flaunt that nonsense to some o' the big's shakin it on the side-walk, they'll drag your teenie butt down an alley and show you what it's for.

They'll tax that thing for hours before they let it up. Are you feelin what I am sayin teenie bopper cuz? I can't believe yer Momma let's you go out with your belly button showin and your pups half hangin out. Man, and those shorts your wearin look like their painted on… leaves nuthin to the imagination."

"God, you guys are too serious", stammered Teisha folding her arms trying to disappear into the upholstery.

"Yeah, I see her GT", tattled Teisha's little brother Gregory, "She's dancing that stuff all around in her underwear to those music videos and checkin it out in the mirror."

Teisha freaked and started smacking Gregory, "You dirty little sneaky rat. You're not supposed to be watchin what I do in my room. I'm tellin mom what you've been up to you little perv!"

"Hey", Sammy yelled turning around looking dead serious, "First, Teisha stop hitting your brother. He don't know any better, but you shouldn't be spying on her either Gregory... that ain't cool. But I was right too Teisha! Ya can't let that nonsense on TV influence how you look, think and talk. Get your head unplugged from that worldly junk!"

Fast Food Served with the Sammy Special

Pulling into the 'Shakes and Burgers' parking lot, there were some guys from the old high school days loitering about. I looked into the rearview and I could see Teisha checking out the bling hanging on some of the less desirable creatures. Turning around I tried to side track Teisha's train of thought and asked, "Taking orders please… what are your preferences?"

"What… we're not getting out", asked Teisha indignantly folding her arms, "Why can't we get out and order what we want? This is so unfair. I thought you guys were really cool. I need to think on it now. There's alotta choices up there on the board."

"Yea, G. T." Gregory said, "I have to think about it too! Man I'm so hungry. We didn't have lunch because of the…" He then stopped short not wanting to bring up the funeral.

Staring through the windshield a creepy feeling came crawling up the back of my neck. Putting up my hand I gestured everybody to quiet down.

Sammy asked, "What's up GT.?"

Pondering our dilemma; should we stay or should we go, I said, "When you leave your home town and go away there are some who wish you well and others who wish you hell. It is also said, you are never more unpopular than you are in your own hometown. Looking over those in attendance here at 'Shakes and Burgers' Sammy there are more of those people who would wish me the latter."

Suddenly the back window rolled down and before I or Sammy could react Teisha sang out like a little tweety bird, "Hey DeShaun, over here honey! How ya doin? Hey, it's me Tiesha Jackson."

Yup, our cover was blown by my ditsy cousin. "Teisha", I said raising my voice, "That guys my age!"

"Isn't that", Sammy asked?

"Yeah Sammy that's the great DeShaun DeCamp from North Lakeland", I said. "Wasn't he", asked Sammy?

"Yup Sammy, he's the one I put down during and after the championship game we won", I answered.

"He's bigger now, ain't he", observed my brother, "You knocked him upside the head with your helmet as I recall right after that game too. He got a couple of friends with him today.

"He did back then too", I reminded him. "After I took him down they all scattered."

"They're kinda big and buff now too. Must have been workin out these past few years", Sammy observed. "We're on the radar now and looks like he's waving at Teisha. But I don't think he knows it's you in the driver's seat... yet. Maybe we should send the kids out for the ice cream, or better idea, just ease it back and leave, what-dya think?"

"Shhheeet", I said, "Yeah he was a junior back then and called unnecessary roughness when the team ran him over going for the win. Ain't no denying the situation Sammy... he's comin this way. The honey pot in the back seat seems to be drawin flies."

"Teisha", Sammy yelled! "What", she answered?

"Remind me to kill you later", Sammy blurted out. "Why", said Teisha, "DeShaun's so cool, you'll like him!"

Sammy and I looked at each other and Sammy said, "Oh yeah Teisha, we're down with his coolness!"

DeShaun didn't even notice us as his eyes were fixed on the prize. He was checkin out the wheels though and as he approached he asked Teisha, "How you doin sweet lady? And where you been hidin all your loveliness? Nice wheels too, who you riden with?"

"My cuz G. T.", Teisha replied, "Just stopped for some ice cream with my little brother and cousins."

"G. T.? Well, introduce me to your cousins sweet thing", DeShaun asked?

Then he stepped back, noted Sammy and eyeballed me sittin in the front seat and exclaimed, "Well if this don't beat all! If I'd known

I would'a invited all my dearest friends along to this party. Shucks girl, I didn't know you were related to royalty!"

DeShaun then turned around waved and yelled to his buddies, "Hey guys we got the great G-T-O right here! And I ain't fakin on this fine ride either! It's here, the real deal!"

DeShaun moved from the passenger side and started coming around to the driver's side. I looked at Sammy and him at me and we both went for the door handles to get out. We weren't staying inside the car at this point, no matter how many there were. "Teisha", I ordered, "Get out of the car and take your brother to get something to eat. Here's twenty bucks… do it now."

She saw from my face that I was dead-on serious, grabbed the money, her little brother and got out of the car. Then I added, "Sit down at a table and wait there until I am ready to leave."

Sammy and I got out of the car and he hurried over to my side. DeShaun came around from the rear and his buddies were now at the front of the car surrounding us.

"Guys", said DeShaun menacingly, "I want you to meet the person who I talk so much about. This is the great G-T-O. He now plays for State and they say he's goin pro. He used to live in this crummy little dirt-ball town. And when he was playin for this little dirt-ball school located in this dirt-ball town they got the break to beat us up for the championship. Fairly or unfairly they did beat us. Isn't that right Mr. G-T effin O?

Sammy started to speak, "Look DeShaun why don't we take this up some…"

"Who the hell is this", asked DeShaun staring at me, moving around to the front of the car with his buddies, "You leavin the dark chocolate Orca speak for you?"

Standing behind DeShaun, Teisha was listening to his comments along with Gregory. While holding an ice cream cone in her hand she decided to jump into the conversation, "I thought you were pretty cool DeShaun! They just buried their father today and now you're pickin on them? Now that I think more about it… it was my mistake to have thought so little of you. You're even a bigger a-hole than I first believed you to be."

Still holding my tongue I listened as DeShaun's cronies now doubled over in laughter at the sprout-dissin' he was taking from Teisha. Seething from the lip-lashing he turned around and said something that he would soon regret, "Look you little skank, why not show me your real talent and take a lick of…!" He didn't get to finish the sentence. Before I knew it Sammy put on DeShaun a professional nose guard hit like I had never seen before.

Sounded like the iron fist of a boxer hitting a body bag when Sammy slammed into DeShaun taking the breath from our once daunting adversary. Both went sailing away; first into a large trash container, but the force of Sammy's delivery kept them moving onto a table where customers were peacefully having lunch. Crossing over it was not a problem; the lubrication of shakes, fries, burgers with relish, ketchup and mustard greased their way. They slid across the picnic table and landed onto the hard cement on the other side.

Little Gregory in the excitement dropped his milkshake and then said, "Cool, looks like heavy weight wrestling on TV!"

Customers scrambled to get out of the way. Then I saw Sammy's head pop up from the other side of the table. He was grinning and said, "Hey, I'm okay!" Looking at the disoriented customers who were staring he stated, "Don't worry folks, I'm a professional… parents, please don't let your kids try this at home!"

When he got up I noticed that DeShaun wasn't moving. "Don't worry folks", Said Sammy, "That guys a professional too but he just needs a nap. He'll be fine and wake up in a few minutes!"

Still I had not said a word. Teisha and Gregory quietly got in the car. As Sammy approached the car, the three guys who looked like they wanted to get into the fight lifted up their hands, shook their heads and disappeared into the crowd. My brother got to the passenger's side, reached for the door handle, stopped and looked at me and asked, "Hungry?", and then quickly answered his own question, "Me neither!"

Finally seated back in the drivers seat I still had not said a word and Sammy suggested, "Let's get in and ride… isn't that what you said less than an hour ago big brother? Well I strongly suggest we do that now before 'Po-Po' arrives."

Starting the engine I drove the car out of the 'Shakes and Burgers' parking lot and headed back to our aunt's house. Teisha had become a quiet little church mouse.

Upon reaching Teisha and Gregory's home they got out and it was Teisha who spoke up, "Thank you guys for the treats and I want to say that I have learned a huge lesson today. You're right Sammy, I need a reality check. Thanks for doing what you did for me."

Gregory then said, "Yeah man… that was like, way cool, even though I dropped my shake. It was worth the ride!" Gregory made a fist and tapped Sammy's and said, "You the true man… the true."

They closed the car door and ran up the steps and their mom was waiting for them. We waved our see ya laters and I let out the clutch.

Sammy looked at me and said, "Ya know, you never shut up! You just keep on yackin away, never let anyone get a word in. You are one rude dog. So why dontchya just keep your big mouth shut!"

Looking over at Sammy who was so full of himself I inquired, "Feelin good?"

"Oh yeah", he said.

"Feelin like you just kicked some righteous butt", I asked?

"Uh, huh", Sammy replied with a wide grin.

"I'm thinkin maybe there had been some justifiable hurtin going on", I added, "Yeah, I am as mad about poppa passin as you are and maybe DeShaun DeCamp was in the right place at the wrong time today. Unfortunately for him, that is the first time I have ever seen you roar into action like that. You musta been holdin that in for a long, long time?"

"Uh, huh", Sammy replied, "Long time comin Yo. It was the dark chocolate comment that set me off though."

"You don't say… just the dark chocolate part", I asked?

"Don't go there", Sammy warned making a fist.

Smiling I looked over at Sammy and he pointed at his head again giving me a nod dangling the keys to poppas shop. "We can still trade you know", Sammy said, "Brains for muscle?"

"I'll keep the car… what say we go out to where poppa got hit", I asked, "Really want to see that place if you can show me?"

"Can do my brutha", answered Sammy, "Momma placed some flowers and a little cross right there alongside the road a few days ago before you got home."

Revelation

Sirens sounded out in the distance. Nervously my brother and I made a zig-zag through the town and came out on the road where poppa had been hit. Suggesting an evasive measure to Sammy I said , "Maybe we should have taken the car back to the toy box, put the tarp over it and went in momma's car."

"Ah, I wouldn't worry about it", said Sammy, "It wasn't you who started the fight. You didn't even say a word. You just stood there with your mouth hangin' wide open while the "Amazing Sammy" body slammed and took the great DeCamp to the ceeement."

Laughing I said, "That's right, the real perp was my quiet little brother, who by the way has chocolate shake, ketchup, mustard and there's even a few fries sticking to your shirt. Poppa wouldn't like it if you got his brand new bucket seats all messed up."

"DeCamps gonna be one hurtin mutha dog when he gets his sense back. Pride and body were tested today", Sammy said providing his take on the situation. "And big brother… in addition from the past to today his vengeance towards the Owens family will be boilin' over."

"You might be right, but first you need to change your clothes if you want to continue to ride with me", I jested.

"Get outta town", Sammy said, "Its right up here on the left… over there's the cross and flowers."

Making a u-turn in the road I came back to the spot and pulled alongside the road. We got out and walked over to the flowers. Sammy pointed out where poppa was found in the vacant lot and told me that his gas can was about twenty five feet further than that.

"He was hit pretty hard G. T. but the police say he didn't die right away. Poppa bled out right where he was laying", Sammy explained, "His van was about a half mile back that way and the gas station is just over there. The lights from the station almost shine this far. He may have been thinking of crossing the street at the time. That must have been when he was hit."

What Sammy and I didn't know was in the exact spot we parked the car was where poppa was hit. In that spot is where the first few drops of our poppa's blood spilled onto the ground. Inanimate objects are supposed to know nothing or feel anything. But behind our backs the G. T. O.'s headlights quarter flashed and the engine seemed to rev up and motor down. Perhaps it was in recognition of the person who served its resurrection? Sammy and I both looked back at the car and then each other. "Must be a wiring glitch", I said. Sammy shrugged his shoulders.

Tears began welling up in my eyes as I looked first down the road in the direction from where poppa left his vehicle to where it was thought he had been hit. No braking skid marks either, as that would show someone had conscience and thought about slowing down… there was no consideration but that of malice that I could see.

"How fast did the cops determine the vehicle was traveling", I asked Sammy.

He looked at the ground and said, "They think from pops weight, the distance he traveled and all, the car they're looking for should have a pretty good dent. They did find some glass which looks to be from a headlight and a small piece of chrome."

"How fast", I again asked?

"Around fifty five, they think", Sammy replied.

"This is a thirty-five mile an hour zone through here", I mumbled and then said, "Had to be kids goofing around. As you said Sammy that's hit and run… hell no, that's premeditated murder. That's first degree manslaughter at least. Whoever did this knows that too. They ran leaving poppa to bleed out over there in that field."

Pensively we stood around looking this way and that and then I asked Sammy, "Did anyone at the gas station see anything or hear anything? What's wrong with this is somebody had to see something, somebody knows exactly what happened and they need to step forward."

"Cops aren't sayin much at this time G. T.", Sammy explained, "The investigation is on-going and they do have some people of interest is all they said."

"Maybe we outta do some investigating of our own", I speculated, "Maybe it was clowns like the ones at 'Shakes and Burgers' today."

All of a sudden a car pulled up alongside and a familiar voice spoke out, "Well as we live and breathe boys… if it ain't the chocolate Orca and his silent partner! You missin your daddy boys. I told you 'Mr. Big Time' I'd catch up with you one day. I guess today's the day. Don't mean to catch you in such an emotionally weakened condition, BUT…"

DeShaun made a sign with his hand and fingers like that of a gun and said, "to you and your poor old hard workin daddy boys."

As he said that we could hear all his cronies in the car having a good hoot. Quickly pulling away they spun the wheels purposely throwing dirt and stones on to our car and knocking over the cross and flowers momma had placed beside the road.

Standing on the roadside, staring at the car speeding away in disbelief, behind our backs, down in the field where poppa drew his last breath something else was going on. Like pea soup coming to a boil, a few bubbles burst forth where poppa's blood had coagulated on the surface of the ground. Again without us noticing the old G. T. O.'s headlights quarter flashed but this time it shivered and shook as if an icy wind had touched it to the very core of its engine block.

Up the street went DeShaun and his wrecking crew, making a u-turn they came back and stopped across the street from us. Revving the engine of the car he yelled, "Want to see if you got the nut of your brother G-T-O? Let's see if you can live up to the rep of what you're drivin… to the strippins young buck!"

DeShauns face took on an evil hue as he menacingly growled, "You and I settle this now once and for all… no interference… everybody else backs off."

Again he rev's the engine and touts, "You first. I'll wait for ya. First one there gets first right of the fight."

"Alright", I yelled. "Enough is enough, we settle this!"

"Come on bro", Sammy says shaking his head, "This is a set up! There are four of them and only two of us."

"Get in the car Sammy", I demanded, "Something tells me if we don't settle this now it never will be."

The Tourniquet

And God said to Abraham, "Kill me a son…"
Abe say, "Man, you must be putting me on…"

God say, "No…"
Abe say, "What…?"

God say, "You can do what you want Abe, but…
The next time you see me comin', you better run…"

"And where do you want this killin' done…"
"Why, out there on highway 61…"

So my brother and I get in the still running car. GTO rev's up and life takes on a whole new meaning. It was something that I never experienced before, in fact, the sound startled Sammy and he commented on it, "What the… do you hear that GT, the car sounds pissed man?"

It did too… about as angry as I was, and I floored the gas pedal. Letting out the clutch the car snapped forward, solid black lines trailed behind. In front of the gas station we turned a one eighty. Tread marks again etched into the road. We pulled up beside DeShaun and he snapped to attention.

Sammy calmly rolled down his window and rendered DeShaun a look and said, "Heard that, felt that too didn't ya?"

DeShaun looked at me and said, "I'm impressed, I'll give ya that… maybe cupcake might know how, but I doubt it. Anybody can do that with the proper horses. Let's see what you do in the real… drive it sweetheart… you got the road… go!"

Dead panned I stared straight ahead, gripping the wheel, paying no attention to the dialogue.

Looking at me Sammy rolled his eyes and said, "You got the road. I sure hope you know what you're doin… cupcake—sweetheart… really… what do you two got goin?"

Business, it was just business now. Popping the clutch, shutting my brother up, we leaped forward leaving DeShaun and the Route 61 road sign in the smoke.

"Wooo… hooo", Sammy exclaimed! He quickly tightened his seat belt and grabbed the *'hold on for dear life bar'* above the door. It was as if the car suddenly became a part of me and we were now an entity all our own. Talk about power, but this was insane. DeShaun was so far behind he appeared like a fly speck on the rearview.

Suddenly the car slowed down all by it-self. Sammy looked at me and said, "Hey the coal strippin's still another five miles… stop foolin around! If we get there first, we can be ready."

Looking into the rearview I saw DeShaun coming up fast. Closer and closer… and I put the pedal down but the car would cough and knock. "I don't know what's happening", I complained in desperation, "Maybe the gas is old and it's clogging the filter?"

Now on top of us, I see DeShaun through the rearview mirror pointing and laughing and he starts blowing the horn and nudging our rear bumper. They pull up beside us. We were doing about sixty and oncoming traffic would soon become an issue. "Hey ladies, what seems to be the problem", He yells out, "You need us to push you the rest of the way?"

Strangely the G TO leaps forward and slows down, taunting, revving, egging DeShaun on over and over again. Sammy punches me in the ribs and says, "Look over there at DeShauns front right quarter panel. Looks like there's a piece of chrome missing… looks like the whole headlight fixture's been changed. Some works been done… paint doesn't match."

"Be the detective later", I yelled, "Right now I am too busy tryin to control this situation."

Still side by side and up ahead there appeared a cattle truck bearing down in the opposite lane. As DeShaun tried slowing down to maneuver behind us, our car slowed down keeping him in harm's way. He tried speeding up and so did our car. He looked over at me and gave me the high sign. The oncoming tractor trailer was now laying on the air horn. Suddenly our car sped forward allowing DeShaun to ease behind us.

Sammy looked at me and asked, "What's up with you? I'm for going along and settling a possible score but it ain't up to us to kill nobody."

"Not in control Sammy", I stammered, and took my hands off the wheel and my foot off the gas.

"Dear God", he said taking in whole the picture and asked, "Whose driving this thing?"

Again and again the car braked allowing them to nudge us. DeShaun pulls up beside us and yells, "Hey fool, what are you doin? Are we gonna to get there or is this going to be a D. O. A.?"

The G. T. O. now slammed on its brakes and pulled directly behind the other car and nudged it. Again both cars are moving in the wrong lane of traffic. The G. T. O. burnt tread pushing against the other car moving forward faster and faster. Passengers in DeShaun's car were staring back at us in horror giving us the hi-sign.

Coming up was a hair pin turn and unknown to us a heavy laden coal truck was chugging up the mountain on the other side. The more DeShaun tried to correct and get to the right side the GTO kept the pressure on pushing him back into the oncoming lane.

Freaking out Sammy yelled, "Knock it off... G. T. YOUR GOING TO GET US ALL KILLED! George T. Owens you have to do something. Do something now! Do it quick!"

"I'm trying Sammy", I yelled, "I am trying but this car..."

In horror Sammy looked at me and I at him and then like the screen on TV when 'Outer Limits' came on everything went to a snowy gray screen with white noise, then we faded to black.

Do we all get what we wish for, like I suggested in the beginning? Some folks have it come true in ways they could never even imagine. Maybe and it is pure supposition that we wanted DeShaun to pay for what he had done? But only if he was the one who had actually killed poppa as Sammy suspected. Only then perhaps a wrong would be righted? But it's not ours to be judge, jury and executioner. Maybe DeShaun begrudged I never play pro football because I lopped him upside the head a little too hard. In this way he too would have his revenge. But cold revenge is not ours to meter out.

Greetings from Tarin Row Correctional

But hold up. See I got this here letter in the mail and from where I'm sittin and lookin back, well... maybe everything was justified. Just not in the way we hoped for or could have imagined.

"Pastor Owens how you been, man", DeShaun asks and says, "Thanks for comin to see me today. It's been awhile."

"Yes it has DeShaun", Pastor Owens agreed and explained. "I've been traveling looking for work, and I wanted to stop by and tell you that even with this bum leg of mine a college has hired me. Says so right here in this acceptance letter. Ya know, to coach our sport of choice. So I'll be movin' on and can't come by for our weekly devotionals anymore.

"You'll be making a difference in young lives Pastor, just like you did in mine", DeShaun stated. "Your forgiveness... your families forgiveness, you don't realize how much your compassion has meant to my life."

"Don't give me all the credit", Pastor Owens pointed out. "It was the good Lord with my Momma's prayers who brought us all around to see things clear. Poppa and Momma always wanted a man of ministry in the family… so here I am in the flesh and bone and now football too."

They both laughed at the complexity of their story and the irony.

"Ya know Pastor", DeShaun said. "Even though I am in here doin time, I am trying… trying hard to bring others, yeah these knuckleheads… through my testimony of course… around to the Word my brother. Speaking of which, howse your brother doin?"

"Oh Sammy's fine… trying to keep up with technology. Everything changes so fast", Pastor Owens stated.

"Not from in here it don't", DeShaun pointed out with a laugh and admitted. "Everyday's the same old story, same old song and dance about how they got the wrong dude… I wasn't even near the place, they say, yet they got'em on video."

"You're making a difference from in here too DeShaun", Pastor Owens remarked, "And that's what it's all about man… taking bad circumstances and tragedy, turning it around and squeezing the best out of life. The good Lord saved us for a reason. I am sorry our lives didn't turn out the way we dreamed, yet here we sit to testify… together. At one time we wanted to kill each other. Hate didn't steal the prize that day and praise God for that", Pastor Owens concluded, "Amen"

"No it didn't Pastor", DeShaun admitted. "But that day… could have been a real different story… it was a miracle wasn't it? I mean, the way you nudged my back quarter panel pushing me into that muddy ditch so I couldn't move. I couldn't open the door until the cops came."

Looking into the distance DeShaun speculated, "If we had gone on with our game, ain't no tellin how it would have ended. But… I mean lives were saved Pastor. Disaster and hell was just around that turn."

"DeShaun you have no idea what it was like being in the GTO that day" Pastor Owens explained. "After we left you we went on down the highway and right before that hair pin turn the wheels came off and everything went sideways… the car literally disassembled right there in the middle of the highway; pieces, parts, I mean doors and tires littered the highway in both directions.

Yeah, that's when I got my leg so messed up. I would never play ball again, but there in front of us was a broken down truck and the highway was blocked right on the other side of that hair pin turn. Anyone coming through from our direction would not have seen it and bang… it would have been all over.

There Sammy and I were left sitting in our seats, in the middle of highway 61. The funny thing though… the car's lights were flashing sending a signal to all approaching cars."

"Life turns on a dime don't it George Taylor Owens", DeShaun said and smiled. "That's how that place got its name you know."

"What do you mean", Pastor Owens asked?

"Tourniquet… that hair pin turn man", DeShaun said. "Maybe you didn't know. People's lives have been left bleeding there dude… so many accidents… so many lives changed, cut off… like a tourniquet stopping the flow man, for good and bad."

"I get it", Pastor Owens states as he hands a small box to DeShaun.

"What's up", DeShaun asked?

"Open it", Pastor Owens urged.

Opening the box DeShaun got a wide grin. "G. T. O., I'll be", and added, "George Taylor Owens, I hope they'll let me keep it."

"Already approved", Pastor Owens said smiling and surmised.

Staring at the key ring DeShaun added. "It was ignorance, stupidity and selfishness that led to what happened and why we sit here today in this place of despair. We were a car load of punks that night when we saw your dad on the side of the road, walking with a gas can in hand. Yeah, we should have stopped and gave him a ride. That would have been the decent Christian and kind thing to do. But the devil was on the playground and he whispered loud and clear, and I made the choice to listen. 'See how close you can come and scare the bee-jeezes out of that old man, it was suggested!' But, the road had a soft shoulder and the front tire dug into it and pulled the car right into your dad. We never meant to hurt him Pastor, let the truth be known. But after we hit him though, all we could think about was to run away, cover it up, keep our mouths shut and play the tough guys. As I confessed before and will continue to confess the fact that

I am truly sorry for the pain I have caused to you, your brother and momma for the rest of my life Pastor Owens."

"I can accept that and forgive. Who knows what God has in his plans for us for the future? If I had gone on to pro-ball maybe I would have got hurt or worse… hooked or strung out trying to keep it up to play the game. God knows what to do with us if we allow Him to do His job and place the ball in His hands. Now, that's how I play it anyway. My times almost up DeShaun, so if you'd be so kind and hand me my walking cane."

"Pastor George Taylor Owens", DeShaun said, "Whodda thunk! It was the life changer that day at 'Shakes and Burgers'. And boy I could use one of those meals now. God bless you G. T. O.

"You too DeShaun DeCamp", Pastor Owens answered back. "I'll write, and we'll speak soon."

The very next day DeShaun was going through the lunch call line when he got stopped before he could enter by a serious looking guard, "DeCamp!"

"Yessir", DeShaun answered.

"Get over here outta line and now. No lunch for you today", the surly guard shouted.

"WHAT!

"NOW DeCAMP!"

Walking over to the guard DeShaun had a hang dog look about him as he held out his hands for the cuffs.

"Want you in the guards mess and that's an order", the guard smirked.

DeShaun entered and there sat Pastor Owens with a huge double order of 'Shake's and Burger's' sitting in front of him. "I wanted our last time together to be a meal and a prayer. So I bribed the guards with some burgers and fries and I brought you a new study Bible and a Concordance. After all I spoke to the powers that be and we all view you as a Minister and a peacekeeper in here."

"I ain't gonna do it", DeShaun stated.

Everyone in the room got a funny look.

"I ain't gonna break down, oh no, ya'll can't do that to me. BUT… I sure am gonna enjoy that wonderful food, so let's have at it. Thought I had done something wrong and was gonna get solitary for a spell. Hey, God is good and all the time, Amen.